Final Faceoff

Helaine Becker

Illustrated by
Sampar

Scholastic Canada Ltd.
Toronto New York London Auckland Sydney
Mexico City New Delhi Hong Kong Buenos Aires

604 King Street West, Toronto, Ontario M5V 1E1, Canada

Scholastic Inc.
557 Broadway, New York, NY 10012, USA

Scholastic Australia Pty Limited
PO Box 579, Gosford, NSW 2250, Australia

Scholastic New Zealand Limited
Private Bag 94407, Greenmount, Auckland, New Zealand

Scholastic Children's Books
Euston House, 24 Eversholt Street, London NW1 1DB, UK

Library and Archives Canada Cataloguing in Publication
Becker, Helaine, 1961-
Final faceoff / Helaine Becker ; illustrated by Sampar.
(Looney Bay all-stars ; 7)
ISBN 978-0-545-99009-7
I. Sampar II. Title. III. Series: Becker, Helaine, 1961- ..
Looney Bay All-Stars ; 7
PS8553.E295532F46 2008   jC813'.6   C2008-901877-X

ISBN-10: 0-545-99009-2

Text copyright © 2008 by Helaine Becker.
Illustrations copyright © 2008 by Scholastic Canada Ltd.
All rights reserved.

If you purchased this book without a cover, you should be aware that
this book is stolen property. It was reported as "unsold and destroyed"
to the publisher, and neither the author nor the publisher has
received any payment for this "stripped book."

No part of this publication may be reproduced or stored in a retrieval system,
or transmitted in any form or by any means, electronic, mechanical, recording,
or otherwise, without written permission of the publisher, Scholastic
Canada Ltd., 604 King Street West, Toronto, Ontario M5V 1E1, Canada. In
the case of photocopying or other reprographic copying, a licence must
be obtained from Access Copyright (Canadian Copyright Licensing Agency),
1 Yonge Street, Suite 800, Toronto, Ontario M5E 1E5 (1-800-893-5777).

6 5 4 3 2 1   Printed in Canada   08 09 10 11 12

Contents

Chapter 1

Reese McSkittles pulled off his hockey gloves. He threw them on the change-room bench and began unlacing his skates. Beside him, his best friend Darren loosened his helmet and wiped the sweat from his forehead.

"That was awesome," Darren said. "Doesn't it seem like ages since we played a normal game like that, without any uninvited guests to mess things up?"

Reese smiled. Darren was right. It *had* been ages. During the past crazy year, the only game in town had been coping with mysterious visitors in Looney Bay. The cause of all the trouble was a magic golden coin Reese had found at that same rink almost one year ago. Whenever Reese rubbed the coin, people from other times appeared! Vikings, knights, gladiators, pirates and explorers had all shown up at one time or another. When time travellers appeared, Reese and his pals wound up in some seriously sticky situations — even once in a battle to the death!

Reese finished changing out of his hockey gear. Resting for a moment, he pulled the coin from the back pocket of his jeans. He always kept it on him now, ever since the time a beetle had landed on it. Rubbing its feet on the coin, the beetle had summoned up a fusty pharaoh from the afterlife.

"Status report?" asked Darren, pointing at the coin. Darren knew that before anything weird happened, the faces on the coin changed.

Reese examined both sides. "It's still the same — an Egyptian ankh on one side and the sphinx on the other," he replied with relief.

Reese tucked the coin back into his pocket.

"That's good," Darren said. "Having to deal with time travellers this weekend would be a royal pain. Our history report on famous explorers is due on Monday. I haven't even started writing mine yet."

"Me neither," said Reese. "Who's yours going to be about?"

"Sir Francis Drake. He sailed around the world back in the sixteenth century. Yours?"

Reese shrugged. "You're one step ahead of me. I haven't even decided yet."

"You'll think of something," Darren

laughed, clapping Reese on the back. "You always do. See ya later — I'm heading to the library right now."

"I'll catch up in a minute," Reese said with a wave.

With Darren gone, the rink was quiet. Reese leaned back and closed his eyes. He tried to plan his report, but his mind kept drifting back to the coin. Strange as it seemed, he had gotten used to being sucked into one wacky adventure after another. What he hadn't gotten used to was worrying about *when* the next one would start.

Reese struggled to get comfortable on the hard bench. Something was digging into him. He shifted on the bench, but the bump was still there. It was starting to really bug him.

What the heck is that? Reese wondered.

He wiggled his bum some more, trying to get comfortable.

No luck. No matter how much he wiggled, or how far he slid down the bench, the bump just kept digging into his left butt cheek.

He ran his hand along the bench's wooden slats, feeling for the mysterious object. There was nothing there.

Uh oh, thought Reese.

He touched his back pocket. The bump was the coin inside it! And it seemed to be pulsing ...

Reese gingerly drew the coin out of his pocket. It was just as he had feared. The coin now showed a sailing ship on one side, and a woman with a ruffled collar and a crown on the other. Letters ran around the outside of the coin. Reese sounded them out.

"R ... E ... G ... I ... N ... A ... E ... L ... I ... Z ... A ... B ... E ... T ... H ..." Reese said out loud. "Elizabeth is a name. But what does 'Regina' mean?" He let his head slump back against the wall. "Whatever it is, it can't be good."

"Of course this isn't good! It's a crisis of the utmost importance! We must act quickly!" came a voice from beside him.

Reese practically jumped out of his skin. It was another time traveller!

Chapter 2

A tall, red-headed lady had appeared out of thin air. She was dressed in an old-fashioned gown with a ruff around the neck. A huge jewelled crown perched on top of her head.

"And for your information, young man, *Regina* is Latin for 'Queen.' As in me, Queen Elizabeth of England," the haughty redhead sniffed.

Reese's heart sank. Just what he

needed — another pushy royal! And if this was the same Queen Elizabeth he thought it might be, she was no ordinary royal — she was the sixteenth century's most powerful ruler!

The Queen stood tapping a pair of white gloves impatiently against her palm. "Do you have news of the

whereabouts of that irritating Sir Francis Drake? He is much needed."

Reese replied, "Er, I'm sorry, Your Highness. But I don't think he's anywhere near here."

"Nonsense. He can't be far. Make haste! The Spanish Armada is assembling off the English coast whilst we speak."

"Maybe," Reese spluttered. "But not this coast. You see, this isn't England. This is Looney Bay. There's nothing off our coast but icebergs and a couple of cod jiggers."

"Do not be insolent!" shouted the Queen. "Did I not see Spanish ships with mine own eyes? Two score or more, ready to storm our shores and end our most illustrious reign!"

Reese sighed. "I guess we'd better

look," he said. "Let's go."

With the Queen right behind him, Reese headed for a nearby bluff. He reached the top and waited politely for the Queen as she picked her way up the path. With his eyes fixed on her face, Reese pointed at the harbour. One glance would be enough to show Queen Elizabeth that she wasn't in Merrye Olde Englande anymore.

"You see?" Reese said. "*Nada* — no Armada."

Queen Elizabeth harrumphed. "Then what would you call all those ships waving the Spanish flag? Plum pudding?"

Reese turned and looked. To his surprise, the harbour was crammed with ships. And all of them were pointing cannons at Looney Bay!

Chapter 3

Reese saw a puff of smoke. A moment later, he heard a high whistling followed by a *CRASH!* A ship had opened fire on the Medieval Faire amusement park!

"The English knights! We have to help them!" shouted Reese. He was thinking of Sir Waverly and Sir Hugh, the time-travelling brothers who had arrived in Looney Bay a few months earlier and who now ran the Faire.

The sky was full of smoke and thunder. Cannonballs rained down around Reese and the Queen as they ran.

"Incoming!" he yelled. He grabbed the Queen's wrist and dove for cover.

"Whew! That was close," Reese said.

"*Pfft*," said the Queen. "Once Drake is found, we'll destroy those Spanish pea-shooters in a trice."

"Yo! Reese!"

It was Darren! He was shielding his head with his backpack and darting across the Faire from cart to cart.

At last Darren made it across to them. He threw himself down beside Reese, breathing hard.

"Let me guess," Darren said. "You rubbed the coin."

"No! I didn't!" Reese protested. But then he remembered the annoying bump on the bench, and how he had waggled his bum with the coin in his back pocket . . . He blushed.

"Er, I might have rubbed it by accident," he said. "But that doesn't matter now. What matters is that lady behind me is Queen Elizabeth from olden days England, and those ships are about to blast the bewillikers out of Looney Bay."

"If she's thinking of mustering an army to stop them, she's just signed up her first recruits," said Darren, pointing over Reese's shoulder.

Sir Waverly and Sir Hugh knelt at the Queen's feet. They were covered in soot and singed around the ears.

"My liege," Sir Waverly was saying. "We are at your service."

"And we'll fight for you, too!" added Sir Hugh.

Reese said, "Quick, Darren — tell me about Sir Francis Drake. The Queen keeps asking for him."

Darren said, "Good thing I went to the library before this all started. I've got a book about him right here." He pulled it from his backpack and flipped to a page marked with a sticky note. "It says Drake was a privateer. That's a kind of pirate. He raided Spanish ships and brought the loot back to England. He was also Vice Admiral of — cool! Your Queen Elizabeth's Navy!"

"Did he have a scraggly blond beard?" asked Reese.

"Uh-huh," replied Darren.

"And a kind of jujube-red face?"

"The book says 'a ruddy complexion,' so I guess so."

"And did he like lawn bowling?" Reese asked.

"Lawn bowling? You've got to be kidding."

"Check it out for yourself," said Reese. "Over there."

Sure enough, a pink-cheeked man with a pointy beard and red-striped breeches was on the lawn in front of the stage. He was hurling a lopsided wooden ball toward a smaller white one and shouting, "Watch your toes, Frobey! This one's gonna be right on the money!"

Darren sighed and nodded. "The other guy must be Martin Frobisher, another privateer and naval commander.

Here's his picture." He held up the book for Reese to see.

"Let's find out if you're right," Reese said. He crawled over to the Queen.

"You know how you were looking for Sir Francis?" he asked. "Is that him over there, with Martin Frobisher?"

As Queen Elizabeth took in the scene, smoke seemed to rise from her ears. "Those irresponsible twits!" she muttered through clenched teeth.

The Queen marched across the square. She grabbed Sir Francis Drake by the ear. Reese couldn't make out her words, but he could see plenty of finger wagging.

Reese's friends Shannon, Laura and Seamus came running up. "What's happening?" Laura asked.

Reese said, "See that lady with the crown? That's Queen Elizabeth I — the sixteenth century's Top Banana. Those are her fave commanders — Sir Francis Drake and Martin Frobisher. And those ships shooting at us? The Spanish Armada — 'armada' means army. Back when Liz was queen, Spain and England didn't get along. They had a really famous war. And it seems like it's about to take place all over again — right here in Looney Bay!"

"A war?" Laura gulped. Another cannonball landed with a crash.

Seamus went white. "Sure seems like it," he said.

"We've got to stop it!" declared Shannon.

"That's not going to be easy," said

Darren. "It looks like the knights have already enlisted the pirates to fight for England. They've rounded up John Cabot and his men too. See?" The Italian explorer and his men had been plucked

from the past earlier that year, and had decided to settle in Looney Bay.

Seamus winced as another cannonball smashed into Galahad's Gifte Shoppe. "That was way too close!"

Queen Elizabeth strode over. Drake and Frobisher followed close on her heels.

"'Tis time to act. My kingdom is at stake!" she said. "Gather round, men!"

The sailors and pirates squeezed around the Queen.

"Drake! You're the highest-ranking commander here. What do you propose to do?"

"I don't know why you're making such a fuss, Bess," Sir Francis whined. "We had plenty of time to finish our bowling game — *and* beat the Spanish."

The Queen rolled
her eyes. "Just get
on with it," she said.
"Frobey and I think
we can take 'em," Sir
Francis said. "If we
can round up a few
ships, we'll send Philip's fleabag fleet
to the bottom of the sea."

"We're pirates, ain't we?" Black-and-
Bluebeard said with a dark gleam in his
eye. "'Course we can get ships."

"No. You
can't," said
Darren flatly.

Black-and-
Bluebeard
bristled.
"Why you . . ."

Reese placed a restraining hand on his arm.

"Not anymore. Remember?" Reese said. "You're in twenty-first century Looney Bay, not your own times. We can't have a naval battle here. That's not the way we do things in Canada anymore. You play by Looney Bay's rules now."

"What do you propose to do, then, little man?" Sir Francis said to Reese. He took out a penknife and started to clean his fingernails with it.

"Explain to the Spanish what I've explained to you," Reese said.

Chapter 4

Halfway across the bay the water grew choppy. Moans emerged from Sir Waverly's helmet.

"Don't tell me a mighty warrior like you gets sea-sick," Reese chuckled.

Sir Waverly groaned.

"Don't worry, there's the Spanish flagship. We'll be aboard in a jiffy."

Reese shouted "Ahoy!" to the sailors on the ship. They tossed down a rope ladder. Reese clambered up.

As soon as Reese reached the deck, a tall Spaniard holding a small white dog in the crook of his arm stepped forward. "I am the Duke of Medina Sedonia, leader of the Spanish Armada.

State your mission," the Duke said, pressing a handkerchief to his lips and turning a peculiar shade of green.

Reese launched into his now familiar explanation of the magic coin. He pointed to an iceberg off to the north-east, and then to Looney Bay. "So you see," Reese concluded, "you're in Newfoundland, Canada. There's really no reason for any shooting."

The Duke turned to look but imme-diately began to sway. He held the hanky even tighter to his lips. Reese narrowed his eyes. Was the Duke, like Sir Waverly, seasick?

An idea popped into Reese's head.

"How about this, Dukie: Come ashore and see for yourself. If you still think you're in England, come back to your ship and we'll battle it out. But if you think you're in Canada, we'll come up with a better way to settle the problems between you and Queen Elizabeth. A *Canadian* way."

The Duke lifted his eyes to the shoreline. There was desperation in his glance.

Another swell lifted, then dropped, the ship.

"You'll let me come ashore, without taking me prisoner?" asked the Duke weakly.

"Yup," Reese replied.

Then, without warning, a sea of armed Spanish soldiers surrounded Reese and the Duke.

"Maybe *he* will, but *we* won't," interrupted a small, trim sailor, his face

shielded by a black scarf.

"That's right," came a second voice, this time from beside Reese.

Reese recognized that voice. But, no ... it couldn't be ...

His hand shot out. He pulled the scarf from the sailor's face. It was Jack Patrick, one of Seamus' old pals from Trinity Bay, their hockey rivals! And the

other was
Roman
Quaig,
another
one of

Seamus' bully-boys!

"Hi, Reesie," sneered Jack. "Fancy meeting you here."

"Wh–what are you doing here?" Reese stammered.

"When you and Seamus got all palsy-walsy, things got pretty boring for us. Then the Duke showed up with this sweet ride. And it turns out that a few of the sailors wanted a captain that didn't throw up every five seconds."

"So Jack led the mutiny," piped up Roman, "and now he's Cap'n Jack."

The Duke let out a whimper. "Oh, it's

true! What will the King of Spain do to me when he finds out I let the ship be taken over?" he wailed, squeezing his little dog tighter.

Reese's eyes narrowed as he looked at Jack and Roman. "So it's you who's been firing at Looney Bay?"

"That's right, Reesie. We've had a most excellent time blowing up bits of Looney Bay," said Jack. "I'm looking forward to wrecking the rest of your 'All-Star' attractions. Won't you be sorry when we blast your beloved arena to smithereens."

Jack let out a scary chuckle. "Now we'll see who's really better: Looney Bay or Trinity Bay."

"It's hardly a fair contest when you're firing on defenceless people," Reese said, thinking fast. "It's not like you're gonna prove anything this way. Only that you're bullies. But we already knew that."

Reese turned to the Duke and said, "Let's go, Dukie. You'll feel better once we get you onto dry land. I'm finished with these two creeps."

"*Muy bien*," the Duke agreed. "Anything to get off this bobbing apple. *Adios, amigos!*"

"Where do you think you're going?" Jack called shrilly. "You can't just leave! I'm not through with you!"

"Yeah, right," snorted Reese as he stepped onto the rope ladder. "You're a bully, Jack, and everyone knows bullies are nothing but cowards underneath."

Reese started down the ladder.

"Oh, yeah?" Jack called down to him.

"Either you stay and fight or my Spanish soldiers will blow Looney Bay to bits."

"I've got a better idea," said Reese. "Tomorrow. Noon. The Looney Bay hockey rink. Your Spanish sailors versus the English and their allies. Let's end this war once and for all."

Chapter 5

Safely back on dry land, the Duke threw himself at Reese's feet and kissed the ground. So did his little dog.

Then the Duke rose, straightened his jacket and cleared his throat.

"Please forgive me," he said. "I am a soldier, not a sailor. I had never been on a ship before

King Philip gave me this command. I tried to refuse, but you do not refuse the King of Spain! I have suffered greatly on this voyage. So has my poor little dog. *Agh*, but I must get back to Spain and report to my King!"

"You won't get the chance unless we stop Jack," said Reese.

The Duke looked like he would burst into tears.

"Don't worry, Dukie. I bet Queen Elizabeth will help."

The Duke drew back in horror. "The English Queen? Here? Now?"

"Uh-huh. And she's hopping mad. It sounds like your King Philip and she don't get along very well."

"No one gets along with Philip. He is a very stubborn royal," said the Duke.

"Aren't they all?" said Reese. "But Queen Elizabeth, at least, is really smart. In the meantime, there's a hockey team I have to train before tomorrow. So let's get cracking!"

By the time they arrived at the Medieval Faire, the Duke had recovered from his seasickness. He strode with purpose into the Castle's Great Hall.

"The Duke of Medina Sedonia, former representative of King Philip of Spain!" Reese announced. The Queen listened carefully as Reese explained what had happened aboard the Spanish ship.

"So we lure your little friends off the ship on the pretext of this amusement you call hockey . . . then we take the sailors hostage and seize the ships! 'Tis an excellent plan, Reese!" crowed the

Queen, clapping her hands in glee.

"But, Your Highness," stammered Reese, "the game's not a pretext! And you can't take the sailors hostage — that wouldn't be right. We play fair here in Looney Bay. The plan is we beat the pants off the Spanish at hockey. You'll defeat King Philip's armada fair and square. And if the English team wins, we've beaten those Trinity Bay bullies once and for all."

A glimmer of admiration crossed the Queen's face.

"You have heart, young Reese," she said. "Go then. Prepare for thy hockey battle."

Chapter
6

Jack and Roman swaggered into the arena. The Spanish sailors trailed behind, looking around them in wonder.

The English were just about to take the ice for warm-up. "I've got an idea!" whispered Sir Francis when he saw the Spaniards enter. "While everyone's here at the rink, how about I go out to the harbour and set fire to all their boats?"

Frobisher gave Sir Francis a high-five.

"Nice plan, good fellow! Worked a charm at Cadiz."

Captain Black-and-Bluebeard rubbed his hands together in glee. A sharp nudge from Reese, however, stopped him cold.

"Aye, that was good piratey thinking, matey," said Black-and-Bluebeard with a sad sigh. "But even pirates like us play fair in Canada."

"Never ye mind, we'll beat the tar out of those fellers anyway," said Frobisher. "Look at  'em skate." He finished lacing his skates and stepped out onto the ice.

"I used to skate on the Thames when it froze in winter," he announced. "I got lots of practice on my first voyage to Labrador, too." He did a beautiful three-turn.

"How about you, Francis?" Frobisher snickered. "Can you skate?" He executed a sharp hockey stop, spraying Sir Francis.

Sir Francis wobbled onto the ice. "You don't survive the seven seas if you have lousy balance." He pushed off with his right foot, then leaned into a perfect spiral. "Ta dah!"

"Methinks our Admirals will succeed, ahem, *admirably*," said Queen Elizabeth, winking at Reese. "Let the game begin!"

* * *

The English got control of the puck first. Black-and-Bluebeard picked it up and passed it to Frobisher, then Frobisher to Drake. Drake lifted his stick for the slapshot, but a Spanish sailor swooped in. With an expert flourish, the Spaniard flicked the puck down the ice. Goal!

In the stands, the All-Stars watched in disbelief. The Spaniards seemed to get every lucky break. And they played like pros too — passing fast and keeping up the pressure.

Seamus' eyes narrowed suspiciously.

"Are these the same guys we saw slipping and sliding on the ice like a pack of seals during warm-up? They've gotten really good, really fast."

"No lie," agreed Reese. "How did Jack teach them how to play like that so fast?"

Back and forth, back and forth went the puck. The Spanish team kept racking up goals. The English, on the other hand, just couldn't score. Every opportunity melted into thin air.

Reese groaned as the buzzer signalled the end of the second period. The Spaniards were winning 7–0!

In the locker room, Queen Elizabeth paced back and forth, her skirts swirling like the winds of a hurricane. She was fuming mad.

Drake and Frobisher sniped at each other, blaming one another for the mess. Captain Black-and-Bluebeard looked like a whipped puppy, wringing his jersey in his hands. Cabot burst into tears.

"Quit your blubbering," the Queen snapped. "You, Drake! Frobisher! You are a disgrace! You let those Spaniards make fools of us! If you don't win this game, then we will lose the war. England — and Canada — will belong to Spain!"

"Oh, no it won't!" interrupted Reese, jumping to his feet. His heart was pounding a mile a minute. "We're Canadians, and you're our Queen, too!"

"Besides, Jack is cheating! I know it," added Seamus.

"What are you saying, Seamus?" Laura asked.

"Those sailors can't have gotten so good so fast. There's only one explanation: Jack has substituted some of the real Marauders — the Trinity Bay hockey team — for some of the sailors. We can't see anyone's faces under the helmets, but I can tell who they are by the way they skate."

"We have to do something! We can't let Jack beat us by cheating!" said Shannon, wringing her hands. "Come on guys, we have to get in there and show 'em that Looney Bay rules the ice!"

"Yeah!" shouted Darren, pumping his fist in the air.

"Suit up, gang!" shouted Laura. "The third period starts in less than fifteen minutes!"

"Let's play!" said Reese, leaping to his feet. "Come on, All-Stars!"

The Queen placed a firm hand on Reese's shoulder.

"On the ice," she intoned, "my

Lieutenant-General Reese McSkittles shall lead you! Know that no Queen has ever commanded more noble or worthy subjects!"

The All-Stars hooted and hollered in agreement.

Chapter 7

The All-Stars took the ice. Even Seamus joined them. Reese, Laura and Shannon were forwards.

Laura and Reese exchanged determined looks. They had to score eight goals to win — in just one period! It was the toughest challenge they had ever faced.

In goal, Darren slapped his stick on the ice. Soon all the All-Stars were beating out a hypnotic rhythm with their sticks that seemed to demand, "Go Team Go! Go Team Go!" The All-Stars' cheer — the cry of the Ring-Necked Loon — rose from all corners of the stands in an electrifying wall of sound.

The puck hit the ice.

Laura passed the puck to Seamus. Seamus carried it across the blue line, then sent it back to Laura. She pivoted and whacked the puck to Reese in the right corner. Seamus had elbowed his way in front of the crease. Reese passed it to him. A flick of Seamus' wrist put the puck in the top shelf. Score!

Again, Laura faced Jack for the drop. This time, Jack won the faceoff, but Reese swooped in to steal the puck. He skated hard toward the Spanish net — it was a breakaway!

The goalie didn't stand a chance. Reese deked around him and the All-Stars scored again!

Time after time, the All-Stars dug deep and came up with a goal. 7–2, 7–3, 7–4, 7–5 . . . ! No game since Team

Canada took on the Russians in 1972 had been as intense.

With four minutes left in the game, Reese got the puck. He swiveled to pass when suddenly he was flat on his back. Tripped by Spain!

"Hard to skate with a broken tibia, hey Reese?" Jack smirked.

Reese seethed with anger. When the clock resumed, he skated hard. He jammed the puck into the net. Goal!

"That was dirty play, Jack," Laura said, skating toward centre ice.

"The Marauders don't give up easily," replied Jack.

The puck dropped. Jack tussled with Laura for possession. Laura jabbed him with her stick.

The whistle blew. Penalty All-Stars!

With less than one minute to play, the All-Stars were down by one goal and short-handed.

"Give it all you've got," Laura urged her team from the penalty box.

At the whis- tle, Reese wrestled the

puck from Jack. He carried it behind the net. Reese passed to Seamus. Seamus tried to shovel the puck into the net.

Blocked!

The puck rocketed right back at Reese. He put his stick down and the puck slammed into it.

It ricocheted off his stick and into the net! Goal!

The final buzzer rang. It was tied, 7-7. There was going to be a shootout!

Roman shot first. Saved by Darren!

Then Sir Francis shot. Wide.

The Spanish first mate's shot didn't even cross the crease.

Next was Reese. He took a deep breath. The goalie looked huge. The net looked tiny.

If he scored, the All-Stars would win

the game. But if he missed . . .

Reese swallowed hard. He had to judge his shot just right.

He started toward the net. He heard nothing but the beating of his own heart. Just a little closer . . . closer . . .

Reese saw his opening. His instincts took over. He snapped his wrists.

The puck rose into the air. It arced gracefully over the goalie's right shoulder. Score! Looney Bay had won the game!

Chapter 8

Sir Waverly ran out onto the ice. He grabbed Jack by the arm. "That's enough of your tricks."

"You, too," said Sir Hugh, grabbing Roman.

The knights dragged the two boys to the All-Stars bench. Queen Elizabeth looked down on them coldly.

"We give up," they mumbled.

"You concede, then, that you are but

spoiled brats, and that you deserve to be locked in the Tower for the rest of your sorry lives?"

"Um, I guess so," said Jack.

"Do with them as you will, Waverly," said the Queen. "If they do not obey you, you may send them to the Tower."

"I've got plenty of work for them before I'm ready to send them to any old tower," Waverly said. "Cleaning up the mess they made of the Medieval Faire amusement park.

You'll be digging and painting and rebuilding every day after school until you're forty-six years old."

As Sir Waverly pulled the boys along, Reese heard Roman say, "We'll be out of school long before we're forty-six, won't we, Jack?"

"And now," said the Queen, "as victor, I naturally wish to return to London."

Sir Francis said, "Me, too."

"Ditto for me," said Frobisher.

"Reese, make it so," ordered the Queen.

Reese took the coin from his pocket.

"I still don't really know how this thing works," he said. "Or even why I got the coin in the first place. But I'll try rubbing it — that's always seemed to work before."

"Here goes nothing!" Reese started rubbing the coin between his thumb and forefinger.

"*Pare!*" interrupted the Spanish first mate with a shout. He came running over and began babbling frantically, grasping at the Duke's hands.

The Duke listened for a moment, shrugged, and turned to the Queen. "He says the men don't wish to go back to Spain. He is begging me to ask you to allow them to stay here. After all, Spain hasn't been a dandy place to live since the Inquisition began."

"*Si, si,*" said the sailor.

"He also says he is sorry for making the mutiny. He promises they will follow my command if I accept their apology," reported the Duke. "They are right — I was not a good captain at sea. But I am very good on land. If they wish to stay here in Looney Bay, I want to stay, too. Then I will not have to go back on the ship, or travel through time again. Both ideas make me sick in the stomach."

Darren shook his head in dismay. "You guys have to go back! How will Looney Bay manage with 40 more ships and 3000 sailors?"

"Don't worry," replied the Duke. "Many of my men, back at home, were fishermen. Good fishermen, who take care of the sea. They will be honest, decent Newfoundlanders."

"*Si*," said the first mate. Then he added in halting English, "All we really

want is to fish — and play soccer."

Cabot's eyes lit up. "Soccer?" he said, clasping his hands in joy. "*Magnifico!*"

Darren remained unconvinced. "This town is already crawling with 'come from aways.' *Far, far,* aways. How many more can we handle?" he said.

Reese shrugged his shoulders. "Canada's almost always welcomed immigrants. That's what makes us such a great country."

"And here, we all get along," Sir

Waverly said pointedly to Jack and Roman. "It's a lesson we all have had to learn."

"That's right!" said Reese. "The pirates, when they first came here, were thieves. But now, they run a successful  — and peaceful — sports business."

"And my brother and I were feuding, until we learned to get along," said Sir Waverly.

Laura said, "I think I'm seeing a pattern here. The Vikings — remember how crude and violent they were before they got here? Now look at them up in Norstead, putting out planters of

daisies in the spring.
Emperor Zero also
learned a thing or two
about ways to have fun,
other than feeding folks to the lions."

"Look at the coin!" shouted Darren. "It's starting to glow!"

And it was — it had brightened in Reese's hand as Laura spoke.

Shannon piped up excitedly. "That's it! Everyone who came to Looney Bay was fighting. But once they got here, they learned to stop! That was the coin's purpose!"

The coin shone even brighter.

"And when Cleo and the Pharaoh got here, they were at

each other's throats. By the time they left, they were all kissy-face!" added Reese. As if in response to his words, the coin pulsed. It even seemed to grow.

Cabot stepped forward, his eyes fixed on the coin. "This is not true of me," he said, touching his heart with his palm. "I am Italian. Like all my people, I am a lover, not a fighter."

The coin dimmed slightly.

Laura replied, "Maybe so, but that still didn't stop you from trying to take Looney Bay from the Beothuks. You weren't exactly on a friendly mission, were you?"

Cabot stroked his chin. "I think I understand. We had to learn to be more understanding of other people. Learn, how you say, to be respectful of cultural differences."

The coin brightened again.

Darren said, "So the whole reason the coin keeps bringing people to Looney Bay is so they can learn to 'play nice'?"

The coin seemed to triple in size.

"But why here?" asked Reese. "And why me?"

"Maybe because *we* needed to learn how to 'play nice,' too," said Laura.

"Laura's right. We didn't exactly get along with everybody in those days," Darren pointed out. "Especially you, Reese. You really hated Seamus, didn't you?"

"Well ..." Reese replied. He looked at the ground to avoid meeting Seamus' eyes.

"But now, we are all like one big happy family," said Cabot, throwing his arms around Darren and Laura. The next thing Reese knew, the pirates, explorers and Spanish sailors were all standing with their arms draped over each other's shoulders, swaying back and forth and singing "Kumbaya."

"Fine," said Darren. "Dukie, you can stay. Your sailors, too."

Reese closed his fist around the coin. It felt warm in his hand.

"Your coin story has been very . . . *illuminating*," said the Queen dryly. "I'll keep it in mind during the rest of my reign, which, with luck, may be a long one."

"With the armada out of the way, it will be," said Reese. "And I'm sure that you will be remembered as one of the greatest queens of all time."

"Would that it be so," replied the Queen. "Now, do you think that glowing coin can send me back to my beloved England?"

"I think so," Reese said hesitantly.

"Very well. Before I go, I will honour

you for what you have done today. Kneel, Reese."

Reese knelt. Queen Elizabeth tapped him on the shoulder with a hockey stick.

"I hereby dub you Sir Reese, Earl of Loondonderry."

Reese rose to his feet. He rubbed the coin between his fingers.

Elizabeth gave a little queenly wave. Nothing happened.

"Oh, for heaven's sake. Give it to me," Elizabeth said. She reached for the coin. As soon as her fingertips touched it, there was a *POP!* The Queen, Sir Francis Drake and Martin Frobisher all disappeared!

Chapter 9

The coin in Reese's hand stopped glowing. It now looked like an ordinary loonie, with a picture of the Queen — Elizabeth II — on one side, and a loon on the other.

Seamus asked, "What are you going to do with the coin, Reese? If our theory is right, we don't need a hunk of metal to help us keep the peace in Looney Bay anymore."

"I have an idea," said Reese. "This all started when I found the coin at the rink, right? The coin should go back to where it came from — here — the rink. It's the heart of Looney Bay, after all."

"Go for it," said Seamus.

Reese skated out to centre ice. He dropped the coin.

For a second, the spinning coin looked like a falling puck. Reese felt his body automatically brace as if for a faceoff. But when the coin hit the ice, it didn't

bounce. Instead, it kept on going, drilling down into the surface of the ice.

Reese peered hard at the ice as the surface melted

back together. The coin was gone. All
Reese could see was the faintest
glimmer of gold coming from some
place far below the ice, as if from
another world. It was as if there had
never been a magic coin or anything
out of the ordinary in Looney Bay.